'There was nothing of the blond beast about the gigolo – he was dark, slim, beautiful as some Latin god. And how soft his eyes were, how sweet his mouth ... Horrible, horrible gigolo!'

JEAN RHYS
Born 24 August 1890, Roseau, Dominica
Died 14 May 1979, Exeter, England

'La Grosse Fifi', 'Vienne', 'Tea with an Artist' and 'Mixing Cocktails' were all first published in *The Left Bank and Other Stories* by Jonathan Cape in 1927.

ALSO PUBLISHED BY PENGUIN BOOKS
After Leaving Mr Mackenzie · *Voyage in the Dark* ·
Good Morning, Midnight · *Wide Sargasso Sea* · *Quartet*

JEAN RHYS

La Grosse Fifi

PENGUIN BOOKS

PENGUIN CLASSICS

Published by the Penguin Group
Penguin Books Ltd, 80 Strand, London WC2R ORL, England
Penguin Group (USA) Inc., 375 Hudson Street, New York, New York 10014, USA
Penguin Group (Canada), 90 Eglinton Avenue East, Suite 700, Toronto, Ontario,
Canada M4P 2Y3 (a division of Pearson Penguin Canada Inc.)
Penguin Ireland, 25 St Stephen's Green, Dublin 2, Ireland (a division of Penguin Books Ltd)
Penguin Group (Australia), 250 Camberwell Road, Camberwell, Victoria 3124, Australia
(a division of Pearson Australia Group Pty Ltd)
Penguin Books India Pvt Ltd, 11 Community Centre, Panchsheel Park,
New Delhi – 110 017, India
Penguin Group (NZ), 67 Apollo Drive, Rosedale, North Shore 0632, New Zealand
(a division of Pearson New Zealand Ltd)
Penguin Books (South Africa) (Pty) Ltd, 24 Sturdee Avenue, Rosebank, Johannesburg 2196,
South Africa

Penguin Books Ltd, Registered Offices: 80 Strand, London WC2R ORL, England

www.penguin.com

Selected from *Tigers Are Better-Looking*, published in Penguin Books 1972
This edition published in Penguin Classics 2011

3

All rights reserved

Typeset by Jouve (UK), Milton Keynes
Printed in England by Clays Ltd, St Ives plc

ISBN: 978-0-141-19620-6

www.greenpenguin.co.uk

Penguin Books is committed to a sustainable future
for our business, our readers and our planet.
The book in your hands is made from paper
certified by the Forest Stewardship Council.

Contents

La Grosse Fifi

'The sea,' said Mark Olsen, 'is exactly the colour of Reckett's blue this morning.'

Roseau turned her head to consider the smooth Mediterranean.

'I like it like that,' she announced, 'and I wish you wouldn't walk so fast. I loathe tearing along, and this road wasn't made to tear along anyhow.'

'Sorry,' said Mark, 'just a bad habit.'

They walked in silence, Mark thinking that this girl was a funny one, but he'd rather like to see a bit more of her. A pity Peggy seemed to dislike her – women were rather a bore with their likes and dislikes.

'Here's my hotel,' said the funny one. 'Doesn't it look awful?'

'You know,' Mark told her seriously, 'you really oughtn't to stay here. It's a dreadful place. Our patronne says that it's got a vile reputation – someone got stabbed or something, and the patron went to jail.'

'You don't say!' mocked Roseau.

'I do say. There's a room going at the pension.'

'Hate pensions.'

'Well, move then, come to St Paul or Juan les Pins – Peggy was saying yesterday . . .'

'Oh Lord!' said Roseau rather impatiently, 'my hotel's all right. I'll move when I'm ready, when I've finished some work I'm doing. I think I'll go back to Paris – I'm getting tired of the Riviera, it's too tidy. Will you come in and have an aperitif?'

Her tone was so indifferent that Mark, piqued, accepted the invitation though the restaurant of that hotel really depressed him. It was so dark, so gloomy, so full of odd-looking, very odd-looking French people with abnormally loud voices even for French people. A faint odour of garlic floated in the air.

'Have a Deloso,' said Roseau, 'It tastes of anis,' she explained, seeing that he looked blank. 'It's got a kick in it.'

'Thank you,' said Mark. He put his sketches carefully on the table, then looking over Roseau's head his eyes became astonished and fixed. He said: 'Oh my Lord! What's that?'

'That's Fifi,' answered Roseau in a low voice and relaxing into a smile for the first time.

'Fifi! Of course – it would be – Good Lord! – Fifi!' His voice was awed. 'She's – she's terrific, isn't she?'

'She's a dear,' said Roseau unexpectedly.

Fifi was not terrific except metaphorically, but she was stout, well corseted – her stomach carefully arranged to form part of her chest. Her hat was large and worn with a rakish sideways slant, her rouge shrieked, and the lids of her protruding eyes were painted bright blue. She wore very long silver earrings; nevertheless her face looked huge – vast, and her voice was hoarse though there was nothing but Vichy water in her glass.

Her small, plump hands were covered with rings, her small, plump feet encased in very high-heeled, patent-leather shoes.

Fifi was obvious in fact – no mistaking her mission in life. With her was a young man of about twenty-four. He would have been a handsome young man had he not plastered his face with white powder and worn his hair in a high mass above his forehead.

'She reminds me,' said Mark in a whisper, 'of Max Beerbohm's picture of the naughty lady considering Edward VII's head on a coin – You know, the "Ah! well, he'll always be Tum-Tum to me" one.'

'Yes,' said Roseau, 'she is Edwardian, isn't she?' For some unexplainable reason she disliked these jeers at Fifi, resented them even more than she resented most jeers. After all the lady looked so good-natured, such a good sort, her laugh was so jolly.

3

She said: 'Haven't you noticed what lots there are down here? Edwardian ladies, I mean – Swarms in Nice, shoals in Monte Carlo! . . . In the Casino the other day I saw . . .'

'Who's the gentleman?' Mark asked, not to be diverted. 'Her son?'

'Her son?' said Roseau, 'Good Heavens, no! That's her gigolo.'

'Her – what did you say?'

'Her gigolo,' explained Roseau coldly. 'Don't you know what a gigolo is? They exist in London, I assure you. She keeps him – he makes love to her, I know all about it because their room's next to mine.'

'Oh!' muttered Mark. He began to sip his aperitif hastily.

'I love your name anyway,' he said, changing the conversation abruptly – 'It suits you.'

'Yes, it suits me – it means a reed,' said Roseau. She had a queer smile – a little sideways smile. Mark wasn't quite sure that he liked it – 'A reed shaken by the wind. That's my motto, that is – are you going? Yes, I'll come to tea soon – sometime: goodbye!'

'He's running off to tell his wife how right she was about me,' thought Roseau, watching him. 'How rum some English people are! They ask to be shocked and

4

long to be shocked and hope to be shocked, but if you really shock them . . . how shocked they are!'

She finished her aperitif gloomily. She was waiting for an American acquaintance who was calling to take her to lunch. Meanwhile the voices of Fifi and the gigolo grew louder.

'I tell you,' said the gigolo, 'that I must go to Nice this afternoon. It is necessary – I am forced.'

His voice was apologetic but sullen, with a hint of the bully. The male straining at his bonds.

'But mon chéri,' implored Fifi, 'may I not come with you? We will take tea at the Negresco afterwards.'

The gigolo was sulkily silent. Obviously the Negresco with Fifi did not appeal to him.

She gave way at once.

'Marie!' she called, 'serve Monsieur immediately. Monsieur must catch the one-thirty to Nice . . . You will return to dinner, my Pierrot?' she begged huskily.

'I think so, I will see,' answered the gigolo loftily, following up his victory as all good generals should – and at that moment Roseau's American acquaintance entered the restaurant.

They lunched on the terrace of a villa looking down on the calmly smiling sea.

'That blue, that blue!' sighed Miss Ward, for such

was the American lady's name – 'I always say that blue's wonderful. It gets right down into one's soul – don't you think, Mr Wheeler?'

Mr Wheeler turned his horn spectacles severely on the blue.

'Very fine,' he said briefly.

'I'm sure,' thought Roseau, 'that he's wondering how much it would sell for – bottled.'

She found herself thinking of a snappy advertisement: 'Try our Bottled Blue for Soul Ills.'

Then pulling herself together she turned to M. Leroy, the fourth member of the party, who was rapidly becoming sulky.

Monsieur Leroy was what the French call 'un joli garçon' – he was even, one might say, a very pretty boy indeed – tall, broad, tanned, clean looking as any Anglo-Saxon. Yet for quite three-quarters of an hour two creatures of the female sex had taken not the faintest notice of him. Monsieur Leroy was puzzled, incredulous. Now he began to be annoyed.

However, he responded instantly to Roseau's effort to include him in the conversation.

'Oh, Madame,' he said, 'I must say that very strong emotion is an excuse for anything – one is mad for the moment.'

'There!' said Roseau in triumph, for the argument

had been about whether anything excused the Breaking of Certain Rules.

'That's all nonsense,' said Mr Wheeler.

'But you excuse a sharp business deal?' persisted Roseau.

'Business,' said Mr Wheeler, as if speaking to a slightly idiotic child, 'is quite different, Miss . . . er . . .'

'You think that,' argued Roseau, 'because it's your form of emotion.'

Mr Wheeler gave her up.

'Maurice,' said Miss Ward, who loved peace, to the young Frenchman, 'fetch the gramophone, there's a good child!'

The gramophone was fetched and the strains of 'Lady, Be Good' floated out towards the blue.

The hotel seemed sordid that night to Roseau, full of gentlemen in caps and loudly laughing females. There were large lumps of garlic in the food, the wine was sour . . . She felt very tired, bruised, aching, yet dull as if she had been defeated in some fierce struggle.

'Oh God, I'm going to think, don't let me think,' she prayed.

For two weeks she had desperately fought off thoughts. She drank another glass of wine, looked at Fifi sitting alone at the mimosa-decorated table with

7

protruding eyes fixed on the door; then looked away again as though the sight frightened her. Her dinner finished she went straight up into her bedroom, took three cachets of veronal, undressed, lay down with the sheet over her head.

Suddenly she got up, staggered against the table, said 'Damn', turned the light on and began to dress, but quietly, quietly. Out through the back door. And why was she dressing anyway? Never mind – done now. And who the hell was that knocking?

It was Fifi. She was wonderfully garbed in a transparent nightgown of a vivid rose colour trimmed with yellow lace. Over this she had hastily thrown a dirty dressing-gown, knotting the sleeves round her neck.

She stared at Roseau, her eyes full of a comic amazement.

'I hope I do not disturb you, Madame,' she said politely. 'But I heard you – enfin – I was afraid that you were ill. My room is next door.'

'Is it?' said Roseau faintly. She felt giddy and clutched at the corner of the table.

'You are surely not thinking of going out now,' Fifi remarked. 'I think it is almost midnight, and you do not look well, Madame.'

She spoke gently, coaxingly, and put her hand on Roseau's arm.

Roseau collapsed on the bed in a passion of tears.

'Ma petite,' said Fifi with decision, 'you will be better in bed, believe me. Where is your chemise de nuit? Ah!'

She took it from the chair close by, looked rapidly with a calculating eye at the lace on it, then put a firm hand on Roseau's skirt to help her with the process of undressing.

'La,' she said, giving the pillow a pat, 'and here is your pocket handkerchief.'

She was not dismayed, contemptuous or curious. She was comforting.

'To cry is good,' she remarked after a pause. 'But not too much. Can I get anything for you, my little one? Some hot milk with rum in it?'

'No, no,' said Roseau, clutching the flannel sleeve, 'don't go – don't leave me – lonely –'

She spoke in English, but Fifi responding at once to the appeal answered:

'Pauvre chou – va,' and bent down to kiss her.

It seemed to Roseau the kindest, the most understanding kiss she had ever had, and comforted she watched Fifi sit on the foot of the bed and wrap her flannel dressing-gown more closely round her. Mistily she imagined that she was a child again and that this was a large, protecting person who would sit there till she slept.

The bed creaked violently under the lady's weight.

'Cursed bed,' muttered Fifi. 'Everything in this house is broken, and then the prices they charge! It is shameful . . .'

'I am very unhappy,' remarked Roseau in French in a small, tired voice. Her swollen eyelids were half shut.

'And do you think I have not seen?' said Fifi earnestly, laying one plump hand on Roseau's knee. 'Do you think I don't know when a woman is unhappy? – I – Besides, with you it is easy to see. You look avec les yeux d'une biche – It's naturally a man who makes you unhappy?'

'Yes,' said Roseau. To Fifi she could tell everything – Fifi was as kind as God.

'Ah! le salaud: ah! le monstre.' This was said mechanically, without real indignation. 'Men are worth nothing. But why should he make you unhappy? He is perhaps jealous?'

'Oh, no!' said Roseau.

'Then perhaps he is méchant – there are men like that – or perhaps he is trying to disembarrass himself of you.'

'That's it,' said Roseau. 'He is trying to – disembarrass himself of me.'

'Ah!' said Fifi wisely. She leant closer. 'Mon enfant,' said she hoarsely, 'do it first. Put him at the door with a coup de pied quelque part.'

'But I haven't got a door,' said Roseau in English, beginning to laugh hysterically. 'No vestige of a door I haven't – no door, no house, no friends, no money, no nothing.'

'Comment?' said Fifi suspiciously. She disliked foreign languages being talked in her presence.

'Supposing I do – what then?' Roseau asked her.

'What then?' screamed Fifi. 'You ask what then – you who are pretty. If I were in your place I would not ask "what then", I tell you – I should find a chic type – and quickly!'

'Oh!' said Roseau. She was beginning to feel drowsy.

'Un clou chasse l'autre,' remarked Fifi, rather gloomily. 'Yes, that is life – one nail drives out the other.'

She got up.

'One says that.' Her eyes were melancholy. 'But when one is caught it is not so easy. No, I adore my Pierrot. I adore that child – I would give him my last sou – and how can he love me? I am old, I am ugly. Oh, I know. Regarde moi ces yeux là!' She pointed to the caverns under her eyes – 'Et ça!' She touched her enormous chest. 'Pierrot who only loves slim women. Que voulez-vous?'

Fifi's shrug was wonderful!

'I love him – I bear everything. But what a life! What a life! . . . You, my little one, a little courage – we will try to find you a chic type, a –'

She stopped seeing that Roseau was almost asleep. 'Alors – I am going – sleep well.'

Next morning Roseau, with a dry tongue, a heavy head, woke to the sound of loud voices in the next room.

Fifi, arguing, grumbling, finally weeping – the gigolo who had obviously just come in, protesting, becoming surly.

'Menteur, menteur, you have been with a woman!'

'I tell you no. You make ideas for yourself.'

Sobs, kisses, a reconciliation.

'Oh Lord! Oh Lord!' said Roseau. She put the friendly sheet over her head thinking: 'I must get out of this place.'

But when an hour afterwards the stout lady knocked and made her appearance she was powdered, smiling and fresh – almost conventional.

'I hope you slept well last night, Madame; I hope you feel better this morning? Can I do anything for you?'

'Yes, sit and talk to me,' said Roseau. 'I'm not getting up this morning.'

'You are right,' Fifi answered. 'That reposes, a day in bed.' She sat heavily down and beamed. 'And then you must amuse yourself a little,' she advised. 'Distract yourself. If you wish I will show you all the places where one amuses oneself in Nice.'

But Roseau, who saw the 'chic type' lurking in Fifi's

eyes, changed the conversation. She said she wished she had something to read.

'I will lend you a book,' said Fifi at once. 'I have many books.'

She went to her room and came back with a thin volume.

'Oh, poetry!' said Roseau. She had hoped for a good detective story. She did not feel in the mood for French poetry.

'I adore poetry,' said Fifi with sentiment. 'Besides, this is very beautiful. You understand French perfectly? Then listen.'

She began to read:

'Dans le chemin libre de mes années
Je marchais fière et je me suis arrêtée . . .

. . .

'Thou hast bound my ankles with silken cords.

. . .

'Que j'oublie les mots qui ne disent pas mon amour,
Les gestes qui ne doivent pas t'enlacer,
Que l'horizon se ferme à ton sourire . . .

. . .

'Mais je t'en conjure, ô Sylvius, comme la plus
humble des choses qui ont une place dans ta
maison – garde-moi.'

13

In other words: you won't be rotten – now. Will you, will you? I'll do anything you like, but be kind to me, won't you, won't you?

Not that it didn't sound better in French.

'Now,' read Fifi,

'I can walk lightly for I have laid my life in the hands of my lover.

. . .

'Chante, chante ma vie, aux mains de mon amant!'

. . .

And so on, and so on.

Roseau thought that it was horrible to hear this ruin of a woman voicing all her own moods, all her own thoughts. Horrible.

'Sylvius, que feras-tu à travers les jours de cet
être que t'abandonne sa faiblesse?
Il peut vivre d'une sourire, mourir d'une parole.
Sylvius, qu'en feras-tu?'

'Have you got any detective stories?' Roseau interrupted suddenly. She felt that she could not bear any more.

Fifi was surprised but obliging. Yes – she had Arsène Lupin, several of Gaston Leroux; also she had 'Shaer-lock 'Olmes'.

Roseau chose *Le Fantôme de l'Opéra*, and when Fifi had left the room, stared for a long time at the same page:

'Sylvius, qu'en feras-tu?'

Suddenly she started to laugh and she laughed long, and very loudly for Roseau, who had a small voice and the ghost of a laugh.

That afternoon Roseau met Sylvius, alias the gigolo, in the garden of the hotel.

She had made up her mind to detest him. What excuse for the gigolo? None – none whatever.

There he was with his mistress in Cannes and his mistress in Nice. And Fifi on the rack. Fifi, with groans, producing a billet de mille when the gigolo turned the screw. Horrible gigolo!

She scowled at him, carefully thinking out a gibe about the colour of his face powder. But that afternoon his face was unpowdered and reluctantly she was forced to see that the creature was handsome. There was nothing of the blond beast about the gigolo – he was dark, slim, beautiful as some Latin god. And how soft his eyes were, how sweet his mouth . . .

Horrible, horrible gigolo!

He did not persist, but looking rather surprised at her snub, went away with a polite murmur: 'Alors, Madame.'

A week later he disappeared.

Fifi in ten days grew ten years older and she came no more to Roseau's room to counsel rum and hot milk instead of veronal. But head up, she faced a hostile and sneering world.

'Have you any news of Monsieur Rivière?' the patronne of the hotel would ask with a little cruel female smile.

'Oh, yes, he is very well,' Fifi would answer airily, knowing perfectly well that the patronne had already examined her letters carefully. 'His grandmother, alas! is much worse, poor woman.'

For the gigolo had chosen the illness of his grand-mother as a pretext for his abrupt departure.

One day Fifi despatched by post a huge wreath of flowers – it appeared that the gigolo's grandmother had departed this life.

Then silence. No thanks for the flowers.

Fifi's laugh grew louder and hoarser, and she gave up Vichy for champagne.

She was no longer alone at her table – somehow she could collect men – and as she swam into the room like a big vessel with all sails set, three, four, five would follow in her wake, the party making a horrible noise.

'That dreadful creature!' said Peggy Olsen one night. 'How does she get all those men together?'

Mark laughed and said: 'Take care, she's a pal of Roseau's.'

'Oh! is she?' said Mrs Olsen. She disliked Roseau and thought the hotel with its clientèle of chauffeurs – and worse – beyond what an English gentlewoman should be called upon to put up with.

She was there that night because her husband had insisted on it.

'The girl's lonely – come on, Peggy – don't be such a wet blanket.'

So Peggy had gone, her tongue well sharpened, ready for the fray.

'The dear lady must be very rich,' she remarked. 'She's certainly most hospitable.'

'Oh, she isn't the hostess,' said Roseau, absurdly anxious that her friend's triumph should be obvious. 'The man with the beard is host, I'm sure. He adores Fifi.'

'Extraordinary!' said Mrs Olsen icily.

17

Roseau thought: 'You sneering beast, you little sneering beast. Fifi's worth fifty of you!' – but she said nothing, contenting herself with one of those sideway smiles which made people think: 'She's a funny one.'

The electric light went out.

The thin, alert, fatigued-looking bonne brought candles. That long drab room looked ghostly in the flickering light – one had an oddly definite impression of something sinister and dangerous – all these heavy jowls and dark, close-set eyes, coarse hands, loud, quarrelsome voices. Fifi looked sinister too with her vital hair and ruined throat.

'You know,' Roseau said suddenly, 'you're right. My hotel is a rum place.'

'Rum is a good word,' said Mark Olsen. 'You really oughtn't to stay here.'

'No, I'm going to leave. It's just been sheer laziness to make the move and my room is rather charming. There's a big mimosa tree just outside the window. But I will leave.'

As the electric light came on again they were discussing the prices of various hotels.

But next morning Roseau, lying in bed and staring at the mimosa tree, faced the thought of how much she would miss Fifi.

It was ridiculous, absurd, but there it was. Just the

sound of that hoarse voice always comforted her; gave her the sensation of being protected, strengthened.

'I must be dotty,' said Roseau to herself. 'Of course I would go and like violently someone like that – I must be dotty. No. I'm such a coward, so dead frightened of life, that I must hang on to some body – even Fifi . . .'

Dead frightened of life was Roseau, suspended over a dark and terrible abyss – the abyss of absolute loss of self-control.

'Fifi,' said Roseau talking to herself, 'is a pal. She cheers me up. On the other hand she's a dreadful-looking old tart, and I oughtn't to go about with her. It'll be another good old Downward Step if I do.'

Fifi knocked.

She was radiant, bursting with some joyful tidings.

'Pierrot is returning,' she announced.

'Oh!' said Roseau interested.

'Yes, I go to meet him at Nice this afternoon.'

'I am glad!' said Roseau.

It was impossible not to be glad in that large and beaming presence. Fifi wore a new black frock with lace at the neck and wrists and a new hat, a small one.

'My hat?' she asked anxiously. 'Does it make me ridiculous? Is it too small? Does it make me look old?'

'No,' said Roseau, considering her carefully – 'I like it, but put the little veil down.'

Fifi obeyed.

'Ah, well,' she sighed, 'I was always ugly. When I was small my sister called me the devil's doll. Yes – always the compliments like that are what I get. Now – alas! You are sure I am not ridiculous in that hat?'

'No, no,' Roseau told her. 'You look very nice.'

Dinner that night was a triumph for Fifi – champagne flowed – three bottles of it. An enormous bunch of mimosa and carnations almost hid the table from view. The patronne looked sideways, half enviously; the patron chuckled, and the gigolo seemed pleased and affable.

Roseau drank her coffee and smoked a cigarette at the festive table, but refused to accompany them to Nice. They were going to a boîte de nuit, 'all that was of the most chic.'

'Ah bah!' said Fifi good-naturedly scornful, 'she is droll the little one. She always wishes to hide in a corner like a little mouse.'

'No one,' thought Roseau, awakened at four in the morning, 'could accuse Fifi of being a little mouse.' Nothing of the mouse about Fifi.

'I'm taking him to Monte Carlo,' the lady announced next morning. She pronounced it Monte Carl'.

'Monte Carlo – why?'

'He wishes to go. Ah! la la – it will cost me something!'

She made a little rueful, clucking noise. 'And Pierrot, who always gives such large tips to the waiters – if he knew as I do what salauds are the garçons de café –'

'Well, enjoy yourself,' Roseau said laughing. 'Have a good time.'

The next morning she left the hotel early and did not return till dinner-time, late, preoccupied.

As she began her meal she noticed that some men in the restaurant were jabbering loudly in Italian – but they always jabbered.

The patron was not there – the patronne, looking haughty, was talking rapidly to her lingère.

But the bonne looked odd, Roseau thought, frightened but bursting with importance. As she reached the kitchen she called in a shrill voice to the cook: 'It is in the *Eclaireur*. Have you seen?'

Roseau finished peeling her apple. Then she called out to the patronne – she felt impelled to do it.

'What is it, Madame? Has anything happened?'

The patronne hesitated.

'Madame Carly – Madame Fifi – has met with an accident,' she answered briefly.

'An accident? An automobile accident? Oh, I do hope it isn't serious.'

'It's serious enough – assez grave,' the patronne answered evasively.

Roseau asked no more questions. She took up the *Éclaireur de Nice* lying on the table and looked through it. She was looking for the 'Fatal Automobile Accident'. She found the headline:

YET ANOTHER DRAMA OF JEALOUSY

Madame Francine Carly, aged 48, of 7 rue Notre Dame des Pleurs, Marseilles, was fatally stabbed last night at the hotel – Monte Carlo, by her lover Pierre Rivière, aged 24, of rue Madame Tours. Questioned by the police he declared that he acted in self-defence as his mistress, who was of a very jealous temperament, had attacked him with a knife when told of his approaching marriage, and threatened to blind him. When the proprietor of the hotel, alarmed by the woman's shrieks, entered the room accompanied by two policemen, Madame Carly was lying unconscious, blood streaming from the wounds in her throat. She was taken to the hospital, where she died without recovering consciousness.

The murderer has been arrested and taken to the Depôt.

Roseau stared for a long time at the paper.

'I must leave this hotel,' was her only thought, and she slept soundly that night without fear of ghosts.

A horrible, sordid business. Poor Fifi! Almost she hated herself for feeling so little regret.

But next morning while she was packing she opened the book of poems, slim, much handled, still lying on the table, and searched for the verse Fifi had read:

'Maintenant je puis marcher légère,
J'ai mis toute ma vie aux mains de mon amant.
Chante, chante ma vie aux mains de mon amant.'

Suddenly Roseau began to cry.

'O poor Fifi! O poor Fifi!'

In that disordered room in the midst of her packing she cried bitterly, heartbroken.

Till, in the yellow sunshine that streamed into the room, she imagined that she saw her friend's gay and childlike soul, freed from its gross body, mocking her gently for her sentimental tears.

'Oh well!' said Roseau.

She dried her eyes and went on with her packing.

Vienne

Funny how it's slipped away, Vienna. Nothing left but a few snapshots.

Not a friend, not a pretty frock – nothing left of Vienna.

Hot sun, my black frock, a hat with roses, music, lots of music –

The little dancer at the Parisien with a Kirchner girl's legs and a little faun's face.

She was so exquisite that girl that it clutched at one, gave one pain that anything so lovely could ever grow old, or die, or do ugly things.

A fragile child's body, a fluff of black skirt ending far above the knee. Silver straps over that beautiful back, the wonderful legs in black silk stockings and little satin shoes, short hair, cheeky little face.

She gave me the songe bleu. Four, five feet she could jump and come down on that wooden floor without a sound. Her partner, an unattractive individual in badly fitting trousers, could lift her with one hand, throw her in the air – catch her, swing her as one would a flower.

At the end she made an adorable little 'gamine's' grimace.

Ugly humanity, I'd always thought. I saw people differently afterwards – because for once I'd met sheer loveliness with a flame inside, for there was 'it' – the spark, the flame in her dancing.

Pierre (a damn good judge) raved about her. André also, though cautiously, for he was afraid she would be too expensive.

All the French officers coveted her – night after night the place was packed.

Finally she disappeared. Went back to Budapest where afterwards we heard of her.

Married to a barber. Rum.

Pretty women, lots. How pretty women here are. Lovely food. Poverty gone, the dread of it – going.

'I call them war material,' said Colonel Ishima, giggling.

He meant women, the Viennese women. But when I asked him about the Geisha – I thought it might be amusing to hear about the Geisha first hand as it were. Europeans are so very contradictory about the subject – he pursed up his mouth and looked prim.

'We don't talk about these people – shameful people.'

However, he added after looking suspiciously at a dish of kidneys and asking what they were:

'The Geisha were good people during the war, patriotic people. The Geisha served Nippon well.'

He meant the Russo-Japanese War. One had visions of big blond Russian officers and slant-eyed girls like exotic dolls stabbing them under the fifth rib, or stealing their papers when they were asleep . . .

Every fortnight the Japanese officers solemnly entertained their following at Sacher's Hotel, and they were entertained one by one in return, because in a mass they were really rather overwhelming.

Of course, there it was – the Japanese had to have a following. To begin with, not one of them could speak the three necessary languages, English, German and French, properly. It meant perpetual translation and arguments. And they were dreadfully afraid of not being as tactful as an Asiatic power ought to be, or of voting with the minority instead of the majority, which would have been the end of them at Tokio.

Si Ishima had his secretary and confidential adviser (that was Pierre) and Hato had his, and Matsjijiri had his, not to speak of three typists, a Hungarian interpreter and various other hangers-on.

Every fortnight they gave a dinner to the whole lot. It began with caviare and ended with Tokayer and Hato singing love songs, which was the funniest thing I ever heard.

He only had one eye, poor dear; the other disappeared during the Russo-Japanese War. He sang in a high bleat, holding tightly on to one foot and rocking backwards and forwards.

He was very vieux jeu, arrière, a Samurai or something, he wore a kimono whenever he could get into it and he loved making solemn proclamations to the delegation. He called them: Ordres du jour.

He made one to the typists, à propos of the temptation of Vienne, which began like this:

'Vous êtes jeunes, vous êtes femmes, vous êtes faibles. Pour l'honneur du Nippon,' etc, etc.

Through some mistake this ordre du jour was solemnly brought to an elderly, moustached French general, whilst the Commission was having a meeting to decide some minor detail of the fate of the conquered country. He opened it and read: 'Vous êtes, jeunes, vous êtes femmes, vous êtes faibles.'

'Merde, alors!' said the general, 'qu' est-ce c'est que ça?'

Hato was a great joy. He despised Europeans heartily. They all did that, exception made in favour of Germany – for the Japanese thought a lot of the German Army and the German way of keeping women in their place. They twigged that at once. Not much they didn't twig.

But they were all bursting with tact and Ishima, immediately after his remark about war material, paid me many flowery compliments. He hoped, he said, to see me one day in Japan. The Lord forbid!

After dinner we went to the Tabarin. He stared haughtily with boot-button eyes at a very pretty little girl, a girl like a wax doll, who was strolling aimlessly about, and who smiled at him very pitifully and entreatingly when she thought I was not looking.

I knew all about her. She had been Ishima's friend, his acknowledged friend – en titre. She really was pretty and young. The odd thing is that the Japanese have such good taste in European women, whereas European taste in Japanese women is simply atrocious, or so the Japanese say.

Well, and Ishima had got rid of her because she was faithful to him. Odd reason.

It happened like this: he had a visit from a friend from Japan – a prince of the blood, who adored plain boiled fish and ate them in a simple and efficient way, holding them up by the tail with one hand and using his fork vigorously with the other. Ishima offered him with eastern hospitality everything he possessed – his suite of rooms at the Sacher and the services of his little friend. But the little friend, thinking perhaps to enhance her value, objected – objected with violence, made a scene in fact, and Ishima, more in sorrow than anger, never saw her again.

He just couldn't get over it.

Pierre told me that one day, after meditating for a long time, he asked: 'Was she mad, poor girl, or would others have done the same?'

Pierre answered cautiously that it depended. The ones with temperament would all have made a fuss if only for pride's sake, and the Viennese have nearly as much temperament as the French, the Hungarians even more. On the other hand, the Germans – enfin, it depended.

Ishima meditated a long time. Then he shook his head and said: 'Tiens, tiens, c'est bizarre!'. . .

I thought of the story that night and hated him. He was so like a monkey, and a fattish monkey which was worse . . .

On the other hand there was Kashua, who looked even more like a monkey and he was a chic type who had rescued another unfortunate bit of war material deserted without a penny by an Italian officer. Not only did Kashua give her a fabulous sum in yen, but also he paid her expenses at a sanatorium for six months – she was consumptive.

There you are! How can one judge!

Kashua came up grinning and bowing and sat with us. He showed me photographs of his wife – she looked a darling – and of his three daughters. Their names meant: Early Rising, Order, and Morning Sun. And he had bought them each a typewriter as a present.

Then, with tears in his eyes and a quaver of pride in his voice – his little son.

'I think your wife is very pretty,' I told him.

He said, grinning modestly: 'Not at all, not at all.'

'And I am sure she will be very happy when you will go back to Japan,' I said.

'Very happy, very happy,' he told me. 'Madame Kashua is a most happy woman, a very fortunate woman.'

I said: 'I expect she is.'

Well, Kashua is a chic type, so I expect she is too.

But I believe my dislike of the Viennese nightplaces started at that moment.

We found a flat – the top floor of General von Marken's house in the Razunoffskygasse, and André shared it with us for a time.

He was a little man, his legs were too short, but he took the greatest trouble to have his suits cut to disguise it.

I mean, with the waist of his coat very high, almost under the arms, the chest padded, decided heels to his shoes.

After all these pains what Tillie called his 'silhouette' was not unattractive.

One could tell a Frenchman, Parisian, a mile off. Quantities of hair which he had waved every week, rather honest blue eyes, a satyr's nose and mouth.

That's what André was, a satyr – aged twenty-four.

He'd stiffen all over when he saw a pretty woman, like those dogs – don't they call them pointers – do when they see a rabbit. His nose would go down over his mouth.

It was the oddest thing to watch him at the Tabarin when there was a particularly good dancer.

He spent hours, all his spare time, I believe, pursuing, searching.

One day walking in the Kärntnerstrasse we saw the whole proceedings – the chase, the hat raising, the snub. He often got snubbed.

He was so utterly without pretence or shame that he wasn't horrid.

He lived for women; his father had died of women and so would he. Voilà tout.

When I arrived in Vienna his friend was a little dancer called Lysyl.

Lysyl and Ossi was her turn – an Apache dance.

She had a wonderfully graceful body, and a brutal peasant's face – and André was torn between a conviction that she wasn't 'chic' enough and a real appreciation of the said grace – he'd lean over the loge when she was dancing, breathing, hard eyes popping out of his head.

One night we went with him to some out-of-the-way music-hall to see her, and after her turn was over she came to visit our loge – on her best behaviour of course.

I took a sudden fancy to her that night – to her grace and her little child's voice saying: 'Ach, meine blumen – André, André. Ich hab' meine blumen vergessen' – so I snubbed André when he started to apologize, I suppose for contaminating me, and told him of course he could bring her back to supper.

We squashed up together in one of those Viennese cabs with two horses that go like hell. She sat in a big coat and little hat, hugging her blumen – in the dark one couldn't see her brute's face.

She really was charming that night.

But next morning, when she came to say good-bye before going, the charm wasn't at all in evidence.

She took half my box of cigarettes, asked by signs how much my dress had cost, 'Why is this woman polite to me,' said her little crafty eyes.

Also, most unlucky of all, she met Blanca von Marken on the stairs.

An hour afterwards Madame von Marken had come to see me, to protest.

Blanca was a jeune fille. Surely I understood . . . I would forgive her, but in Vienna they were old-fashioned . . .

Of course I understood, and against all my sense of fairness and logic apologized and said I agreed.

For God knows, if there's one hypocrisy I loathe more than another, it's the fiction of the 'good' woman and the 'bad' one.

André apologized too, but I'm sure he had no sense of being wanting in logic.

So he grovelled with gusto, feeling chivalrous as he did so, and a protector of innocence. Oh, Lord!

'Vous savez, mon vieux, je n'ai pas pensé – une jeune fille!'

However, not being Don Quixote I did not even try to protect Lysyl.

I think she could take care of herself.

But though she got on as a dancer and became mondäne Tänzerin – I think that's how they spell it – André was done with her.

The fiat had gone forth.

Elle n'a pas de chic.

Because I liked Blanca and Madame von Marken, I even tried to make up for the shock to their virtue by hanging up Franz Josef and all the ancestors in the sitting-room.

I'd taken them all down in an effort to make the place less gloomy and whiskery and antimacassary – but I saw it hurt that poor pretty lady so up they went again and I started living in my bedroom, which was charming.

Very big, polished floor, lots of windows, little low tables to make coffee – some lovely Bohemian glass.

Also I spent much time in the Prater.

Quantities of lilac, mauve and white –

Always now I'll associate lilac with Vienna.

The Radetsky Hotel was perhaps twenty minutes or half an hour from Vienna by car – and it was real country.

But that is one of the charms of the place – no suburbs.

It wasn't really comfortable; there wasn't a bathroom in the whole establishment, but for some reason it was exciting and gay and they charged enormous prices accordingly.

All the men who made money out of the 'change came there to spend it, bringing the woman of the moment.

All the pretty people with doubtful husbands or no husbands, or husbands in jail (lots of men went to jail – I don't wonder. Every day new laws about the exchange and smuggling gold).

Everybody, in fact.

Very vulgar, of course, but all Vienna was vulgar.

Gone the 'Aristokraten'.

They sat at home rather hungry, while their women did the washing.

The ugly ones.

The pretty ones tried to get jobs as mondäne Tänzerinnen.

Quite right too – perhaps.

Just prejudice to notice podgy hands and thick ankles – keep your eyes glued on the pretty face.

Also prejudice to see stark brutality behind the bows and smiles of the men.

Also prejudice to watch them eat or handle a tooth-pick.

Stupid too – so much better not to look.

The girls were well dressed, not the slightest bit made up – that seemed odd after Paris.

Gorgeous blue sky and green trees and a good orchestra.

And heat and heat.

I was cracky with joy of life that summer of 1921.

I'd darling muslin frocks covered with frills and floppy hats – or a little peasant dress and no hat.

Well, and Tillie was a queen of the Radetzky. It was through her (she told André) that we got to know of it.

Tillie possessed wonderful eyes, grey-blue – hair which made her look like Gaby Deslys, a graceful figure.

And with that she made one entirely forget a dreadful complexion, four gold teeth, and enormous feet.

This sounds impossible in a place where competition was, to say the least of it, keen, but is strictly true.

Every time one saw Tillie one would think – 'Gee, how pretty she is.' In the midst of all the others everyone would turn to look at her and her gorgeous hair.

And behind walked André, caught at last, held tight 'by the skin', as the French say.

All his swank was gone – he watched her as a dog watches his master, and when he spoke to her his voice was like a little boy's.

She'd flirt outrageously with somebody else (half the men there had been her lovers so it was an exciting renewal of old acquaintanceships), and André would sit so miserable that the tears were nearly there.

One night in fact they did come when I patted him on the arm and said 'Poor old André – cheer up.'

'Une grue,' said Pierre brutally, 'André is a fool – and Frances, leave that girl alone –'

But I didn't leave her alone at once, too interested to watch the comedy.

Next Saturday evening we were dining at Radetzky with a German acquaintance of Pierre's.

Excessively good-looking, but, being a Prussian, brutal, of course.

'Donner-r-r- wetter-r-r-' he'd bawl at the waiters, and the poor men would jump and run.

But perhaps I exaggerated the brutality for he'd done something I'm still English enough to loathe: he'd discussed Tillie with great detail and openness – he'd had a love affair with her.

Just as we were talking about something else, herself and André hove in sight.

André walked straight to our table and asked if they might join us.

Impossible to refuse without being brutal, though Pierre wasn't cordial, and the other man kissed her hand with a sneer that gave the whole show away.

As for Tillie, she behaved perfectly – not a movement, not the flicker of an eyelash betrayed her – though it must have been trying, just as she was posing as a mondaine, to meet this enemy openly hostile.

Nor did she let it interfere in the slightest with her little plan for the evening, well thought out, well carried out.

She owned a beautiful necklace which she always wore, and that night she firmly led the conversation in the direction of pearls.

I couldn't do much 'leading', or indeed much talking in German. I gathered the drift of things, and occasionally Pierre translated.

Tillie's pearls (she told us) were all she had left of a marvellous stock of jewels (wunderschön!).

In fact, all she had between herself and destitution, all and all –

Ach – the music chimed in a mournful echo . . .

She was sad that evening, subdued, eyes almost black, voice sweet and quivery.

After dinner she asked me charmingly if I would mind 'a little walking' – it was so hot – they weren't playing well.

I was quite ready – it was hot – and Tillie went up to her room and came down with a scarf very tightly wrapped round her throat.

We set out. Myself, Pierre and Lieutenant – I've

completely forgotten his name – walking together, André and Tillie some little way in front.

Pitch dark in the woods round the hotel – so dark that it frightened me after a while, and I suggested going back.

Shouted to the others, no answer, too far ahead.

We'd got back and were sitting comfortably in the hall drinking liqueurs (alone, for everybody assembled in the bar after dinner to dance) when André came in running, out of breath, agitated.

'The pearls, Tillie's pearls, lost – Bon Dieu de bon Dieu. She's dropped them –'

He spoke to me, the only sympathetic listener.

Then entered Tillie. Gone the pathos. She looked ugly and dangerous with her underlip thrust out.

A torrent of German to Pierre who listened and said in a non-committal way: 'She says that André kissed her in the woods and was rough, and that the clasp of the pearls wasn't sure. It's André's fault, she says, and he'll have to pay up.'

The other man laughed. Suddenly she turned on him like a fury.

'Mein lieber Herr . . .' I couldn't understand the words; I did the tone.

'Mind your own business if you know what's good for yourself.'

Meanwhile Pierre, whose instinct is usually to act while other people talk, had gone off and come back with two lanterns and a very sensible proposition.

We would go at once, all four of us, holding hands so that not an inch of the ground should be missed, over exactly the same road.

Too dark for anyone else to have picked them up.

Tillie, to my astonishment, didn't seem very keen.

However, we set out in a long row stooping forward. André held one lantern, Pierre the other.

I looked at first perfectly seriously, straining my eyes.

Then André moved his lantern suddenly and I saw Tillie's face. She was smiling, I could swear – she certainly wasn't looking on the ground.

I looked at Pierre – his search was very perfunctory; the other man wasn't even pretending to look.

At that moment I liked André – I felt sorry for him, akin to him.

He and I of the party had both swallowed the story; we were the Fools.

I could have shaken his hand and said: 'Hail, brother Doormat, in a world of Boots.'

But I'd been too sure of the smile to go on looking.

After that I gave all my attention to the little game the German was playing with my hand.

He'd reached my wrist – my arm – I pulled away –

My hand again, but the fingers interlocked.

Very cool and steady he was – and a tiny pulse beating somewhere.

A dispute. We didn't come this way Tillie was saying.

But it had become a farce to everybody but the faithful André.

We went back, but before we'd come within hearing of the music from the hotel, he had comforted her with many promises.

And he kept them too. He turned a deaf ear to all hints that it was or might be a trick.

When we went to Budapest Tillie came. Later on to Berlin, she went too.

She never left him till she could arrange to do so, taking with her every sou he possessed, and a big diamond he'd bought.

This sequel we heard only later.

Poor André! Let us hope he had some compensation for forgetting for once that 'eat or be eaten' is the inexorable law of life.

The next girl, perhaps, will be sweet and gentle. His turn to be eater.

Detestable world.

★

Simone and Germaine, two of the typists at the delegation, were having a succès fou. Simone at least
deserved it.

She specialized in English, Americans and French.

Germaine on the other hand had a large following
among the Italians, Greeks, and even a stray Armenian
who (she said) had offered her fifty thousand francs for
one night.

Simone was sublimely conceited.

She told me once that Captain La Croix had called
her the quintessence of French charm, Flemish beauty
and Egyptian mystery. (She was born in Cairo, French
mother, Belgian father.)

Both girls looked at me a little warily, but they were
too anxious to keep in with Pierre to be anything but
polite. I'd noticed people growing more and more defer-
ential to Pierre, and incidentally to me. I'd noticed that
he seemed to have money – a good deal – a great deal.

He made it on the 'change, he told me.

Then one day in the spring of 1921 we left the flat in
Razunoffskygasse for rooms in the Imperial.

We sent off the cook and D—, promoted to be my
maid, came with us.

Nice to have lots of money – nice, nice. Goody to
have a car, a chauffeur, rings, and as many frocks as
I liked.

Good to have money, money. All the flowers I wanted. All the compliments I wanted. Everything, everything.

Oh, great god money – you make possible all that's nice in life. Youth and beauty, the envy of women, and the love of men.

Even the luxury of a soul, a character and thoughts of one's own you give, and only you. To look in the glass and you think I've got what I wanted.

I gambled when I married and I've won.

As a matter of fact I wasn't so exalted really, but it was exceedingly pleasant.

Spending and spending. And there was always more.

One day I had a presentiment.

Pierre gave an extra-special lunch to the Japanese officers, Shogun, Hato, Ishima and Co.

We lunched in a separate room, which started my annoyance, for I preferred the restaurant, especially with the Japanese, who depressed me.

It was rather cold and dark and the meal seemed interminable.

Shogun in the intervals of eating enormously told us a long history of an officer in Japan who 'hara-kari'd' because his telephone went wrong during manoeuvres.

Rotten reason I call it, but Shogun seemed to think him a hero.

Escaped as soon as I could upstairs.

I was like Napoleon's mother suddenly: 'Provided it lasts.'

And if it does not? Well, thinking that was to feel the authentic 'cold hand clutching my heart'.

And a beastly feeling too – let me tell you.

So damned well I knew that I could never be poor again with courage or dignity.

I did a little sum; translated what we were spending into francs – into pounds – I was appalled. (When we first arrived in Vienna the crown was thirteen to the franc – at that time it was about sixty.)

As soon as I could I attacked Pierre.

First he laughed, then he grew vexed.

Frances, I tell you it's all right. How much am I making? A lot.

How much exactly? Can't say. How? You won't understand.

Don't be frightened, it – brings bad luck. You'll stop my luck.

I shut up. I know so well that presentiments, fears, are unlucky.

'Don't worry,' said Pierre, 'soon I will pull it quite off and we will be rich, rich.'

45

We dined in a little corner of the restaurant.

At the same table a few days before we came, a Russian girl twenty-four years of age had shot herself.

With her last money she had a decent meal and then bang! Out –

And I made up my mind that if ever it came to it I should do it too.

Not to be poor again. No and No and No.

So darned easy to plan that – and always at the last moment – one is afraid. Or cheats oneself with hope.

I can still do this and this. I can still clutch at that or that.

So-and-So will help me.

How you fight, cleverly and well at first, then more wildly – then hysterically.

I can't go down, I won't go down. Help me, help me!

Steady – I must be clever. So-and-So will help.

But So-and-So smiles a worldly smile.

You get nervous. He doesn't understand, I'll make him –

But So-and-So's eyes grow cold. You plead.

Can't you help me, won't you, please? It's like this and this –

So-and-So becomes uncomfortable; obstinate.

No good.

I mustn't cry, I won't cry.

And that time you don't. You manage to keep your head up, a smile on your face.

So-and-So is vastly relieved. So relieved that he offers at once the little help that is a mockery, and the consoling compliment.

In the taxi still you don't cry.

You've thought of someone else.

But at the fifth or sixth disappointment you cry more easily.

After the tenth you give it up. You are broken – no nerves left.

And every second-rate fool can have their cheap little triumph over you – judge you with their little middle-class judgement.

Can't do anything for them. No good.

C'est rien – c'est une femme qui se noie!

But two years, three years afterwards. Salut to you, little Russian girl, who had pluck enough and knowledge of the world enough, to finish when your good time was over.

The day before we left Vienna for Budapest was thundery and colder.

I'd spent nearly two hours in a massage place the Russian girl had told me of.

The Russian girl was introduced to me to replace Tillie. She had two advantages: a husband, and a slight
knowledge of French.

We'd sat up night after night in the Radetzky bar.
(Pierre always gathered swarms of people round him.)
The most amusing of the party being an old lady over
seventy who wore a bright-yellow wig. She'd been an
actress and still had heaps of temperament left.

There she sat night after night, drinking punch and
singing about Liebe and Frauen with the best.

I came out of the shop and walked down the strasse –
face like a doll's – not a line, not a shadow, eyes nicer
than a doll's. Hadn't I had stuff dropped in to make the
pupils big and black?

Highly pleased with everything I was that afternoon –
with the massage place, with the shortness of my frock,
with life in general.

Abruptly the reaction came when I sat down to dinner. I was alone that evening – the presentiment, the
black mood, in full swing.

A gentleman with a toothpick gazed fondly at me (in
the intervals of serious excavating work), I glued my
eyes on my plate.

Oh, abomination of desolation, to sit for two hours
being massaged, to stand for hours choosing a dress. All
to delight the eyes of the gentleman with the toothpick.

(Who finding me unresponsive has already turned his attention elsewhere.)

I hate him worse than ever.

Franzi is in the hall. The Herr has told him to bring the car and take me for a drive.

Nice Franzi.

I climb in – go quick, Franzi. Schnell – eine andere platz neit Prater neit weg zum Baden – neit Weiner Wald.

This is my German after two years! I mean go fast. Go to a new place, not the Prater, not the way to Baden –

Yes, that night was the last frenzied effort of my guardian angel, poor creature. I've never seen so clearly all my faults and failures and utter futility. I've never had so strong a wish to pack my trunks and clear.

Clear off – different life, different people.

Work.

Go to England – be quite different.

Even clearly and coldly the knowledge that I was not being sincere.

That I didn't want to work.

Or wear ugly clothes.

That for ten years I'd lived like that – and that except for a miracle, I couldn't change.

'Don't want to change,' defiantly.

I've compensations.

Oh, yes, compensations – moments.

No one has more.

'Liar, Liar,' shrieked the angel, 'pack your trunks and clear.' Poor angel – it was hopeless. You hadn't a chance in that lovely night of Vienne.

Especially as in the midst of it came a terrific bump.

In his zeal to find an andere weg Franzi had taken me along a road that hadn't been repaired since the year dot. We'd gone right over a stone, so big that I jumped, not being solid, a good three feet into the air. Fell back luckily into the car.

Franzi has stopped and looks behind frightened. I tell him to go home.

It's not my fault.

Men have spoilt me – always disdaining my mind and concentrating on my body. Women have spoilt me with their senseless cruelties and stupidities. Can I help it if I've used my only weapon?

Yes, my only one.

Lies everything else – lies –

Lord, how I hate most women here, their false smiles, their ferocious jealousies of each other, their cunning – like animals.

They are animals, probably. Look at all the wise men who think so and have thought so.

Even Jesus Christ was kind but cold and advised having as little as possible to do with them.

Besides, if I went back to London –

I go back to what, to who?

How lonely I am – how lonely I am.

Tears.

Self-pity, says the little thing in my brain coldly, is the most ridiculous and futile of emotions. Go to bed, woman.

I creep in and am comforted. How I adore nice sheets; how good the pillow smells.

I'm awfully happy really – why did I suddenly get the blues?

Tomorrow I'll see Budapest.

Ridiculous idea to go to London. What should I do in London –

Goodbye Vienna, the lilac, the lights looking down from Kahlenberg, the old lady with the yellow wig singing of Frauen.

Will I ever be like that old lady? And run to the massage shop because I have to prop up the failing structure? Possibly, probably.

Lovely Vienna. Never see you again.

Nice linen sheets.

Sleep.

Well, we all have our illusions. God knows it would be difficult to look in the glass without them.

I, that my life from seventeen to twenty-two is responsible for my damned weakness, and Simone that she has the prettiest legs in Paris. Good women that they're not really spiteful, bad ones that they're not really growing older or the latest lover growing colder.

I can't imagine winter in Budapest. Can't imagine it anything else but hot summer.

Heat and a perpetual smell, an all-pervading smell – in the hotels, in the streets, on the river, even outside the town I still imagined I smelt it.

The Hungarians told us it used to be the cleanest city in Europe till the Bolsheviks made it dirty – the Bolsheviks and 'the cursed, the horrible Roumanians'.

It was now being cleaned gradually – very gradually, I should say.

Haughton used to bark loudly (he did bark!) about the exact reasons why it had always been, and still was the most interesting city in Europe, with the exception of Petersburg before the war. 'Les femmes ici ont du chien' – that's how the French officers explained the matter.

Anyway, I liked it – I liked it better than Vienna.

Haughton lived in the same hotel as we did. We took our meals together and every night we made up a party for the Orpheum or one of the dancing places. He generally brought along a bald Italian with kind brown eyes, a sailor, and a Polish woman and her husband.

He was in the Commission because he spoke Russian, German, French, Italian, even a little Hungarian. Marvellous person!

He had lived in Russia for years, tutor or something to one of the Grand Dukes, and I admired his taste in ladies. He liked them slim, frail, graceful, scented, vicious, painted, charming – and he was chic with them from first to last – un-English in fact, though he remained English to look at.

But sometimes he spoilt those perfect nights when we dined outside Buda with his incessant, not very clever cynicisms.

'Ha, ha, ha! Good Lord! Yes. Damn pretty woman. What?'

When the tziganes were playing their maddest and saddest – he'd still go on happily barking. . . .

Budapest looks theatrically lovely from a distance. I remember the moon like a white bird in the afternoon sky; the greyish-green trunks of sycamore trees, the appalling bumps in the road.

'Not too fast, Franzi; don't go too fast!' . . .

Then back to the city and its vivid smells, the wail of tzigane orchestras, the little dancer of the Orpheum –

what was her name? . . . Ilonka – nice name, sounds like a stone thrown into deep water. She would come smiling and silent – she could speak neither French nor German – to sit with us when her turn was over.

'Awfully monotonous this tzigane stuff, what?' Haughton would say, fidgeting.

It was, I suppose. It seemed to be endless variations and inversions of a single chord – tuneless, plaintive, melancholy; the wind over the plain, the hungry cry of the human heart and all the rest of it . . . Well, well . . .

There was a hard, elegant, little sofa in our room, covered with striped yellow silk – sky-blue cushions. I spent long afternoons lying on that sofa plunged in a placid dream of maternity.

I felt a calm sense of power lying in that dark, cool room, as though I could inevitably and certainly draw to myself all I had ever wished for in life – as though I were mysteriously irresistible, a magnet, a Femme Sacrée.

One can become absorbed . . . exalted . . . lost as it were, when one is going to have a baby, and one is extremely pleased about it.

One afternoon Pierre said: 'If anyone comes here from the Allgemeine Verkehrsbank you must say that I'm not in and that you don't know when I'll be back.'

Someone called from the bank – a fat, short man, insisting, becoming rude in bad French. He would see Monsieur. He must see Monsieur. Madame could not say when Monsieur would be back. 'Très bien – très bien.' He would go to Monsieur's office to make inquiries.

He departed. His back looked square, revengeful – catastrophic – that's the word. I believe that looking at the man's back I guessed everything, foresaw everything.

I attacked Pierre as soon as he came home. I mean questioned him – but he was so evasive that I turned it into an attack. Evasion has always irritated me.

'Tell me, for Heaven's sake, have you lost a lot of money, or something? You have. I know you have – you must tell me.'

He said: 'My dear, let me alone, I'll pull it off if you let me alone – but I don't want to talk about it . . . Haughton has asked us to dine at the Ritz. . . . Et qu'importent les jours pourvu que les nuits soient belles?'

He made a large and theatrical gesture.

I let him alone, weakly, I suppose. But one gets used to security and to thinking of one's husband as a money-maker, a juggler, performing incredible and mysterious feats with yen, with lire, with francs and sterling . . . 'change on Zurich . . .

I let him alone – but I worried. I caught Haughton

looking at me as if he were sorry for me . . . Sorry for me. Haughton!

Ten days after the man of the Bank had called, I went up to my bedroom at half-past six to change my frock and found Pierre sitting on the striped yellow sofa hunched up, staring at the revolver in his hand.

I always hated revolvers, little, vicious, black things. Just to look at a revolver or a gun gives me a pain deep down in my head; not because they're dangerous – I don't hate knives – but because the noise of a shot hurts my ears.

I said: 'Oh, Pierre, put that thing away! How horribly unkind you are to frighten me!'

Stupid to cry at the very moment one should keep calm.

He was silent, rather surly.

Well, I dragged the truth out of him. He told me, moving one foot restlessly and looking rather like a schoolboy, that he had lost money – other people's money – the Commission's money – Ishima had let him down . . .

Then followed the complicated history of yens – of francs – of krönen. He interrupted himself to say: 'You don't understand a thing about money. What is the good of asking me to explain? I'm done, I tell you, tried everything . . . no good! I may be arrested any time now.'

I was calm, cool, overflowing with common sense. I believe people who are badly wounded must be like that before the wound begins to hurt . . . Now then, what is the best way to stop this bleeding? . . . Bandages . . . Impossible that this and no other is the shot that is going to finish one . . .

I sat on the sofa beside him and said: 'Tell me how much you need to put yourself straight? I can understand that much at any rate.'

He told me, and there was a dead silence.

'Leave me alone,' he said. 'Let me put a bullet in my head. You think I want to go to jail in Budapest? I haven't a chance!'

I explained, still calmly and reasonably, that he must not kill himself and leave me alone – that I was frightened – that I did not want to die – that somehow I would find the money to pay his debts.

All the time I was speaking he kept his eyes on the door as if he were watching for it to open suddenly and brutally. Then repeated as if I had not spoken: 'I'm fichu . . . Go away and let me get out of it the only way I can . . . I've saved four thousand francs ready for you . . . And your rings . . . Haughton will help you . . . I'm fichu . . .'

I set my mouth: 'You aren't. Why can't you be a man and fight?'

'I won't wait here to be arrested,' he answered me sulkily, 'they shan't get me, they shan't get me, I tell you.'

My plan of going to London to borrow money was already complete in my head. One thinks quickly sometimes.

'Don't let's wait then. Pierre, you can't do such a rotten thing as to leave me alone?'

'Mon petit,' he said, 'I'm a damn coward or I would have finished it before. I tell you I'm right – I'm done. Save yourself . . . You can't save me!'

He laughed with tears in his eyes. 'My poor Francine, wait a bit . . .'

'Let's go, let's get away,' I said, 'and shut up about killing yourself. If you kill yourself you know what will happen to me?'

We stared at each other.

'You know damn well,' I told him.

He dropped his eyes and muttered: 'All right – all right! . . . Only don't forget I've warned you, I've told you. It's going to be hell . . . You're going to blame me one day for not getting out quick and leaving you to save yourself.'

He began to walk restlessly up and down the room.

We decided that we could leave early the next morning. Just to go off. Like that. We made plans – suddenly we were speaking in whispers . . .

We had dinner upstairs that night, I remember – paprika, canard sauvage, two bottles of Pommery.

'Allons, Francine, cheer up! Au mauvais jeu il faut faire bonne mine.'

I've always loved him for these sudden, complete changes of mood. No Englishman could change so suddenly – so completely. I put out my hand, and as I touched him my courage, my calm, my insensibility left me and I felt a sort of vague and bewildered fright. Horrible to feel that henceforth and for ever one would live with the huge machine of law, order, respectability against one. Horrible to be certain that one was not strong enough to fight it.

'Au mauvais jeu bonne mine' . . . A good poker face, don't they call it? . . . The quality of not getting rattled when anything goes wrong . . .

When we opened our second bottle of Pommery I had become comfortingly convinced that I was predestined – a feather on the sea of fate and all the rest. And what was the use of worrying – anyway? . . .

As I was drinking a fourth glass, hoping to increase this comforting feeling of irresponsibility, Haughton knocked and came in to see us.

There was a moment that night when I nearly confided in Haughton.

Pierre had gone away to telephone, to see the

chauffeur, and I've always liked those big men with rather hard blue eyes. I trust them instinctively – and probably wrongly. I opened my mouth to say: 'Haughton, this and that is the matter ... I'm frightened to death, really ... What am I to do?'

And as I was hesitating Pierre came back.

At one o'clock we began to pack, making as little noise as possible. We decided to take only one trunk.

I remember the table covered with cigarette ends and liqueur glasses, the two empty bottles of champagne, and the little yellow sofa looking rather astonished and disapproving.

At half-past six in the morning we left the hotel.

That journey to Prague was like a dream. Not a nightmare; running away can be exhilarating but endless as are certain dreams, and unreal.

While I dressed and finished packing my hands had trembled with fright and cold, but before we left Budapest behind us the hunted feeling had vanished.

There is no doubt that running away on a fresh, blue morning can be exhilarating.

I patted the quivering side of the car, gazed at Franzi's stolid back, wondered if he guessed anything, and decided he probably did, sung 'Mit ihrem roten

Chapeau'. After all, when one is leaving respectability behind one may as well do it with an air.

The country stretched flatly into an infinite and melancholy distance, but it looked to me sunlit and full of promise, like the setting of a fairy tale.

About noon we passed through a little plage on the Danube; it must have been Balaton, and there were groups of men and girls walking about in short bathing-suits. Nice their brown legs and arms looked and the hair of the girls in the fierce sun.

Pierre called out: 'Hungry?'

I said: 'Yes.'

But I grew uneasy again when we stopped for lunch at some little village of which I was never to know the unpronounceable name.

Through the open door of the restaurant the village looked bleak in the sunlight and pervaded with melancholy; flocks of geese, countless proud geese, strolled about; several old women sat on a long, low stone bench under a lime tree, on another bench two or three old men. The old women were really alarming. Their brown, austere faces looked as though they were carved out of some hard wood, the wrinkles cut deep. They wore voluminous dark skirts, handkerchiefs tied round their heads, and they sat quite silent, nearly motionless. How pitiless they would be, those ancient ones, to a sinner of their own sex – say a thief – how fiercely they would punish her. Brrrrr! Let us not think of these things.

Pierre said: 'What a life they must have, these people!'

I agreed: 'Dreadful!' looked away from the stone bench, drank my horrible coffee, and went outside. There was a girl, a maid of the inn perhaps, or a goose-girl, going in and out of the back door, carrying pails and tubs. She wore a white bodice so thin that one could plainly see the shape of her breasts, a dark skirt, her feet were bare, her head was small, set on a very long neck, her eyes slanted like Ishima's – I watched her with an extraordinary pleasure because she was so slim and young and finely drawn. And because I imagined that when she glanced at me her eyes had the expression of some proud, wild thing – say a young lioness – instead of the usual stupid antagonism of one female looking at another.

I said to Pierre: 'Oh, I do think that Hungarians can be lovely; they beat the Austrians hollow.'

He answered so indifferently: 'Another type,' that I began to argue.

'The Austrians are always trotting out their rotten old charm that everybody talks about. Hate people who do that. And they're fat and female and rusé and all the rest.'

'Oh!' said Pierre, 'and if you think that Hungarians aren't rusé, my dear, zut! – they are the most rusé of the lot, except the Poles.'

I insisted: 'In a different way . . . Now look at that girl; isn't she lovely, lovely?'

'Un beau corps,' judged Pierre. 'Come on, Francine, let's get off if you are ready.'

I heard the apprehension in his voice and climbed into the car a little wearily. A grind . . . and we had left behind us that goose-girl out of a fairy tale against her background of blue distances quivering with heat.

I began to plan my triumphant return to Hungary with money to pay Pierre's debts. I saw myself sitting at the head of a long table handing little packets of notes to everyone concerned, with the stern countenance of a born business woman: 'Will you sign this, please?'

Then I must have slept, and when I woke I'd begun to feel as if the flight had lasted for days, as though I could not remember a time when I hadn't been sitting slightly cramped, a little sick, watching the country fly past and feeling the wind in my face.

Pierre turned and asked if I were tired or cold.

'No, I'm all right . . . Are you going to drive? Well, don't go too fast . . . don't break our necks after all this.'

We left the flat country behind and there was a sheer

drop on one side of the road. The darkness crept up, the wind was cold. Now I was perfectly sure that it was all a dream and could wait calmly for the moment of waking.

We flitted silently like ghosts between two rows of dark trees. I strained my eyes to see into the frightening mystery of the woods at night, then slept again and the car had stopped when I woke.

'What is it?'

'The frontier . . . keep still . . .'

An unexpected fuss at the frontier. There was a post. A number of men with rifles round a wood fire, an argument which became very loud and guttural. Our passports were produced: 'Kommission – Kurrier.'

'What is it, Pierre?'

He got out of the car without answering and followed one of the men into the shelter.

It was horrible waiting there in the night for what seemed hours, my eyes shut, wondering what jail would be like.

Then Pierre reappeared, still arguing, and got in beside me.

He muttered: 'Je m'en fiche, mon vieux,' and yelled to the chauffeur.

The car jumped forward like a spurred horse. I imagined for one thrilling moment that we would be fired on, and the nape of my neck curled itself up. But when I looked back over my shoulder I saw the knot of men by the light of the fire looking after us as if they were puzzled.

'Frightened?'

'No, only of being sent back. What was it? Had they been told to stop us?'

'No, but nobody is supposed to pass. The frontier is shut, something has happened.'

I said: 'What can it be, I wonder,' without the slightest interest.

'Well,' said Pierre, 'here is Czechoslovakia, and good-bye Hungary!'

'Good-bye, Hungary!' Tears were in my eyes because I felt so tired, so deathly sick.

'You're awfully tired, aren't you, Frances?'

'A bit. I'd like to rest. Let's stop soon. Where will we spend the night?'

'At Presburg. We're nearly there.'

I huddled into a corner of the car and shut my eyes.

It was late when we found a room in the Jewish quarter of the town. All the good hotels were full; and in the hardest, narrowest bed I have ever imagined I lay down and was instantly asleep.

Next morning something of the exhilaration had

come back. We went out to breakfast and to buy maps. It had been decided that we would go to Prague and there sell the car, and then . . .

'I want to go to Warsaw,' announced Pierre.

I said dismayed: 'Warsaw? but, my dear . . .'

The coffee was good, the rolls fresh; something in the air of the clean, German-looking little town had given me back my self-confidence.

I began to argue: 'We must go to London . . . in London . . .'

'Mon petit,' said Pierre, lighting his pipe, 'I don't believe in your friends helping us. I know how naïve you are. Wait, and you will see what your famous friends are worth. You will be roulée from the beginning to the end. Let's go to Warsaw. I believe I can arrange something from there; Francine, do what I say for once.'

I told him obstinately that I did not like Poles. He shrugged his shoulders.

We found the car and Franzi waiting at the hotel.

'Off we go,' said Pierre, cheerfully, 'en route! Here's the brandy flask.'

The road was vastly better, but I had no comforting sensation of speed, of showing a clean pair of heels. Now we seemed to be crawling, slowly and painfully, ant-like, across a flat, grey and menacing country.

I pictured that dreary flatness stretching on and on for miles to the north of Russia, and shivered.

I kept repeating to myself: 'I won't go and be buried in Poland . . . I won't go . . . I don't care . . . I will not . . .'

The wind was cold; it began to drizzle persistently.

'Pierre, we're off the road, I'm sure. That woman put us wrong. This is only a cattle-track.'

It was. And time was wasted going backwards. Pierre cursed violently all the while. He had begun to be in a fever of anxiety to reach Prague.

The walls of the bedroom where we slept that night were covered with lurid pictures of Austrian soldiers dragging hapless Czechoslovakians into captivity. In the restaurant downstairs a pretty girl, wearing a black cape lined with vivid purple, sat talking to two loutish youths. She smoked cigarette after cigarette with pretty movements of her hands and arms and watched us with bright blue, curious eyes.

We drank a still wine, sweetish, at dinner. It went to my head and again I could tell myself that my existence was a dream. After all it mattered very little where we went. Warsaw, London. . . . London, Warsaw . . . Words! Quite without the tremendous significance I had given them.

It was still raining when we reached Prague at last. We made the dreary round of the hotels; they were all full, there were beds in the bathrooms of the Hotel du Passage; it was an hour before we discovered a room in a small hotel in a dark, narrow street.

Pierre began to discuss the sudden return of King Karl to Hungary. We heard the news at the Passage.

That was the trouble at the frontier, of course.

I said indifferently – I was lying down – 'Yes, probably'.

Karl – the Empress Zita – the Allies – Commission – the Whites – the Reds – Pierre himself . . . shadows! Marionnettes gesticulating on a badly lit stage, distracting me from the only reality in life . . . the terrible weight that bowed me down . . . the sickness that turned me cold and mounted up to cloud my brain.

Pierre advised me to have some strong coffee. He rang the bell and a short, fat waiter appeared who looked at me with that peculiar mixture of insolence, disdain, brutality and sentimentality only to be found amongst those of German extraction.

Then he departed to fetch the coffee.

It was an odd place, that hotel, full of stone passages and things. I lay vaguely wondering why Prague reminded me of witches . . . I read a book when I was a kid – *The Witch of Prague.* No. It reminded me of witches anyhow. Something dark, secret and grim.

'I think Prague is a rum place,' I told Pierre. 'What's that bell that keeps ringing next door?'

'A cabaret, cinema perhaps . . . Listen, Frances, it's just the best of luck for us, that business of Karl. Nobody will worry about me just now. Ishima will be far too busy voting with the majority . . . Sacré little Japanese!'

'Probably,' I agreed.

He asked me if I felt ill, suggested a doctor.

'A Czech doctor, my God!'

I pulled the sheets over my head. I only wanted to be left alone, I told him.

'Francine,' said he gently, 'don't be a silly little girl. The doctors are good here if you want one.'

He put the rug over me: 'Rest a bit while I go and see about the car. We'll dine at the Passage and find a place for dancing afterwards. Yes?'

I emerged from under the sheets to smile because his voice sounded so wistful, poor Pierre.

About six that evening I felt suddenly better and began to dress.

Because I noticed at lunch that the grand chic at Prague seemed to be to wear black I groped in the trunk for something similar, powdered carefully, rouged my mouth, painted a beauty spot under my left eye.

I was looking at the result when Pierre came in.

'My pretty Francine, wait a bit! I have something here to make you chic . . . but chic . . .'

He felt into his pocket, took out a long case, handed it to me.

'Pierre!'

'Nice hé?'

'Where did you get them?'

He did not answer.

I looked from the pearls to his dark, amused face, and then I blushed – blushed terribly all over my face and neck. I shut the case and gave it back to him and said: 'How much money have we got left?' And he answered without looking at me: 'Not much; the worst is this war-scare. Czechoslovakia is going to mobilize. It won't be so easy to sell the car. We must sell it before we can move. Never mind, Francine.'

I said: 'Never mind!' Then I took the case, opened it, clasped the pearls round my neck. 'If we're going the whole hog, let's go it. Come on.'

One has reactions, of course.

Difficult to go the whole hog to leave respectability behind with an air, when one lies awake at four o'clock in the morning – thinking.

'Francine, don't cry . . . what is it?'

'Nothing . . . Oh! do let me alone . . .'

When he tried to comfort me I turned away. He had suddenly become a dark stranger who was dragging me over the edge of a precipice . . .

It rained during the whole of the next week, and I spent most of the time in the hotel bedroom staring at the wallpaper. Towards evening I always felt better and would start to think with extraordinary lucidity of our future life in London or Paris – of unfortunate speculation and pearls – of a poker face and the affair of King Karl . . .

One day at the end of our second week in Prague Pierre arrived with two tickets which he threw on the bed: 'There you are, to Liège, to London . . . I sold it and did not get much; I tell you.' . . .

I spent an hour dressing for dinner that night. And it was a gay dinner.

'Isn't the chef d'orchestre like a penguin?'

'Yes, ask him to play the Saltimbanques Valse.'

'That old valse?'

'Well, I like it . . . ask him . . . Listen, Pierre, have we still got the car?'

'Till tomorrow.'

'Well, go to the garage and get it. I'd like to drive like hell tonight . . . Wouldn't you?'

He shrugged: 'Why not?'

Once more and for the last time we were flying between two lines of dark trees, tops dancing madly in the high wind.

'Faster! Faster! Make the damn thing go!'

We were doing a hundred.

I thought: he understands – began to choose the tree we would crash against and to scream with laughter at the old hag Fate because I was going to give her the slip.

'Get on! . . . get on! . . .'

We slowed up.

'You're drunk, Frances,' said Pierre severely.

I got out, stumbled, laughed stupidly – said: 'Good-bye! Poor old car,' gathered up the last remnants of my dignity to walk into the hotel . . .

It was: 'Nach London!'

Tea with an Artist

It was obvious that this was not an Anglo-Saxon: he was too gay, too dirty, too unreserved and in his little eyes was such a mellow comprehension of all the sins and the delights of life. He was drinking rapidly one glass of beer after another, smoking a long, curved pipe, and beaming contentedly on the world. The woman with him wore a black coat and skirt; she had her back to us.

I said: 'Who's the happy man in the corner? I've never seen him before.'

My companion who knew everybody answered: 'That's Verhausen. As mad as a hatter.'

'Madder than most people here?' I asked.

'Oh, yes, really dotty. He has got a studio full of pictures that he will never show to anyone.'

I asked: 'What pictures? His own pictures?'

'Yes, his own pictures. They're damn good, they say' . . . Verhausen had started out by being a Prix de Rome and he had had a big reputation in Holland and

Germany, once upon a time. He was a Fleming. But the old fellow now refused to exhibit, and went nearly mad with anger if he were pressed to sell anything.

'A pose?'

My friend said: 'Well, I dunno. It's lasted a long time for a pose.'

He started to laugh.

'You know Van Hoyt. He knew Verhausen intimately in Antwerp, years ago. It seems he already hid his pictures up then . . . He had evolved the idea that it was sacrilege to sell them. Then he married some young and flighty woman from Brussels, and she would not stand it. She nagged and nagged: she wanted lots of money and so on and so on. He did not listen even. So she gave up arguing and made arrangements with a Jew dealer from Amsterdam when he was not there. It is said that she broke into his studio and passed the pictures out of the window. Five of the best. Van Hoyt said that Verhausen cried like a baby when he knew. He simply sat and sobbed. Perhaps he also beat the lady. In any case she left him soon afterwards and eventually Verhausen turned up, here, in Montparnasse. The woman now with him he had picked up in some awful brothel in Antwerp. She must have been good to him, for he says now that the Fallen are the only women with souls. They will walk on the necks of all the others in Heaven . . .' And my friend concluded: 'A rum old bird. But a bit of a back number, now, of course.'

I said: 'It's a perverted form of miserliness, I suppose. I should like to see his pictures, or is that impossible? I like his face.'

My friend said carelessly: 'It's possible, I believe. He sometimes shows them to people. It's only that he will not exhibit and will not sell. I dare say Van Hoyt could fix it up.'

Verhausen's studio was in the real Latin Quarter which lies to the north of the Montparnasse district and is shabbier and not cosmopolitan yet. It was an ancient, narrow street of uneven houses, a dirty, beautiful street, full of mauve shadows. A policeman stood limply near the house, his expression that of contemplative stupefaction: a yellow dog lay stretched philosophically on the cobblestones of the roadway. The concierge said without interest that Monsieur Verhausen's studio was on the quatrième à droite. I toiled upwards.

I knocked three times. There was a subdued rustling within . . . A fourth time: as loudly as I could. The door opened a little and Mr Verhausen's head appeared in the opening. I read suspicion in his eyes and I smiled as disarmingly as I could. I said something about Mr Van Hoyt – his own kind invitation, my great pleasure.

Verhausen continued to scrutinize me through huge spectacles: then he smiled with a sudden irradiation, stood away from the door and bowing deeply, invited me to enter. The room was big, all its walls encumbered on the floor with unframed canvases, all turned with their backs to the wall. It was very much cleaner than I had expected: quite clean and even dustless. On a table was spread a white cloth and there were blue cups and saucers and a plate of gingerbread cut into slices and thickly buttered. Mr Verhausen rubbed his hands and said with a pleased, childlike expression and in astonishingly good English that he had prepared an English tea that was quite ready because he had expected me sooner.

We sat on straight-backed chairs and sipped solemnly.

Mr Verhausen looked exactly as he had looked in the café, his blue eyes behind the spectacles at once naïve and wise, his waistcoat spotted with reminiscences of many meals.

But a delightful personality – comfortable and comforting. His long, curved pipes hung in a row on the wall; they made the whole room look Dutchly homely. We discussed Montparnasse with gravity.

He said suddenly: 'Now you have drunk your second cup of tea you shall see my pictures. Two cups of tea all English must have before they contemplate works of art.'

He had jumped up with a lightness surprising in a

bulky man and with similar alacrity drew an easel near a window and proceeded to put pictures on it without any comment. They were successive outbursts of colour: it took me a little time to get used to them. I imagine that they were mostly, but not all, impressionist. But what fascinated me at first was his way of touching the canvases – his loving, careful hands.

After a time he seemed to forget that I was there and looked at them himself, anxiously and critically, his head on one side, frowning and muttering to himself in Flemish. A landscape pleased me here and there: they were mostly rough and brilliant. But the heads were very minutely painted and . . . Dutch! A woman stepping into a tub of water under a shaft of light had her skin turned to gold.

Then he produced a larger canvas, changed the position of the easel and turned to me with a little grunt. I said slowly: 'I think that is a great picture. Great art!'

. . . A girl seated on a sofa in a room with many mirrors held a glass of green liqueur. Dark-eyed, heavy-faced, with big, sturdy peasant's limbs, she was entirely destitute of lightness or grace.

But all the poisonous charm of the life beyond the pale was in her pose, and in her smouldering eyes – all its deadly bitterness and fatigue in her fixed smile.

He received my compliments with pleasure, but with

the quite superficial pleasure of the artist who is supremely indifferent to the opinion that other people may have about his work. And, just as I was telling him that the picture reminded me of a portrait of Manet's, the original came in from outside, carrying a string bag full of greengroceries. Mr Verhausen started a little when he saw her and rubbed his hands again – apologetically this time. He said: 'This, Madame, is my little Marthe. Mademoiselle Marthe Baesen.'

She greeted me with reserve and glanced at the picture on the easel with an inscrutable face. I said to her: 'I have been admiring Mr Verhausen's work.'

She said: 'Yes, Madame?' with the inflexion of a question and left the room with her string bag.

The old man said to me: 'Marthe speaks no English and French very badly. She is a true Fleming. Besides, she is not used to visitors.'

There was a feeling of antagonism in the studio now. Mr Verhausen fidgeted and sighed restlessly. I said, rather with hesitation: 'Mr Verhausen, is it true that you object to exhibiting and to selling your pictures?'

He looked at me over his spectacles, and the suspicious look, the look of an old Jew when counting his money, came again into his eyes.

'Object, Madame? I object to nothing. I am an artist.

But I do not wish to sell my pictures. And, as I do not wish to sell them, exhibiting is useless. My pictures are precious to me. They are precious, most probably, to no one else.'

He chuckled and added with a glint of malice in his eyes: 'When I am dead Marthe will try to sell them and not succeed, probably. I am forgotten now. Then she will burn them. She dislikes rubbish, the good Marthe.'

Marthe re-entered the room as he said this. Her face was unpowdered but nearly unwrinkled, her eyes were clear with the shrewd, limited expression of the careful housewife – the look of small horizons and quick, hard judgements. Without the flame his genius had seen in her and had fixed for ever, she was heavy, placid and uninteresting – at any rate to me.

She said, in bad French: 'I have bought two artichokes for . . .' I did not catch how many sous. He looked pleased and greedy.

In the street the yellow dog and the policeman had vanished. The café opposite the door had come alive and its gramophone informed the world that:

> Souvent femme varie
> Bien fol est qui s'y fie!

79

It was astonishing how the figure of the girl on the sofa stayed in my mind: it blended with the coming night, the scent of Paris and the hard blare of the gramophone. And I said to myself: 'Is it possible that all that charm, such as it was, is gone?'

And then I remembered the way in which she had touched his cheek with her big hands. There was in that movement knowledge, and a certain sureness: as it were the ghost of a time when her business in life had been the consoling of men.

Mixing Cocktails

The house in the hills was very new and very ugly, long and narrow, of unpainted wood, perched oddly on high posts, I think as a protection from wood ants. There were six rooms with a veranda that ran the whole length of the house . . . But when you went up there, there was always the same sensation of relief and coolness – in the ugly house with the beginnings of a rose garden, after an hour's journey by boat and another hour and a half on horse-back, climbing slowly up . . .

On the veranda, upon a wooden table with four stout legs, stood an enormous brass telescope. With it you spied out the steamers passing: the French mail on its way to Guadeloupe, the Canadian, the Royal Mail, which should have been stately and was actually the shabbiest of the lot . . . Or an exciting stranger!

At night one gazed through it at the stars and pretended to be interested . . . 'That's Venus . . . Oh, is that Venus, . . . And that's the Southern Cross . . .' An unloaded shotgun leant up in one corner; there were always plenty of straw rocking-chairs and a canvas hammock with many cushions.

From the veranda one looked down the green valley sloping to the sea, but from the other side of the house one could only see the mountains, lovely but melancholy as mountains always are to a child.

Lying in the hammock, swinging cautiously for the ropes creaked, one dreamt . . . The morning dream was the best – very early, before the sun was properly up. The sea was then a very tender blue, like the dress of the Virgin Mary, and on it were little white triangles. The fishing boats.

A very short dream, the morning dream – mostly about what one would do with the endless blue day. One would bathe in the pool: perhaps one would find treasure . . . Morgan's Treasure. For who does not know that, just before he was captured and I think hung at Kingston, Jamaica, Morgan buried his treasure in the Dominican mountains . . . A wild place, Dominica. Savage and lost. Just the place for Morgan to hide his treasure in.

It was very difficult to look at the sea in the middle of the day. The light made it so flash and glitter: it was necessary to screw the eyes up tight before looking. Everything was still and languid, worshipping the sun.

The midday dream was languid too – vague, tinged

with melancholy as one stared at the hard, blue, blue sky. It was sure to be interrupted by someone calling to one to come in out of the sun. One was not to sit in the sun. One had been told not to be in the sun . . . One would one day regret freckles.

So the late afternoon was the best time on the veranda, but it was spoiled for all the rest were there . . .

So soon does one learn the bitter lesson that humanity is never content just to differ from you and let it go at that. Never. They must interfere, actively and grimly, between your thoughts and yourself – with the passionate wish to level up everything and everybody.

I am speaking to you; do you not hear? You must break yourself of your habit of never listening. You have such an absent-minded expression. Try not to look vague . . .

So rude!

The English aunt gazes and exclaims at intervals: 'The colours . . . How exquisite! . . . Extraordinary that so few people should visit the West Indies . . . That *sea* . . . Could anything be more lovely?'

It is a purple sea with a sky to match it. The Caribbean. The deepest, the loveliest in the world . . .

Sleepily but tactfully, for she knows it delights my father, she admires the roses, the hibiscus, the humming birds. Then she starts to nod. She is always falling asleep, at the oddest moments. It is the unaccustomed heat.

I should like to laugh at her, but I am a well-behaved little girl ... Too well-behaved ... I long to be like Other People! The extraordinary, ungetatable, oddly cruel Other People, with their way of wantonly hurting and then accusing you of being thin-skinned, sulky, vindictive or ridiculous. All because a hurt and puzzled little girl has retired into her shell.

The afternoon dream is a materialistic one ... It is of the days when one shall be plump and beautiful instead of pale and thin: perfectly behaved instead of awkward ... When one will wear sweeping dresses and feathered hats and put gloves on with ease and delight ... And of course, of one's marriage: the dark moustache and perfectly creased trousers ... Vague, that.

The veranda gets dark very quickly. The sun sets: at once night and the fireflies.

A warm, velvety, sweet-smelling night, but frightening and disturbing if one is alone in the hammock. Ann Twist, our cook, the old obeah woman has told me: 'You all must'n look too much at de moon ...'

If you fall asleep in the moonlight you are bewitched, it seems ... the moon does bad things to you if it shines on you when you sleep. Repeated often ...

So, shivering a little, I go into the room for the comfort of my father working out his chess problem from the *Times Weekly Edition*. Then comes my nightly duty mixing cocktails.

In spite of my absentmindedness I mix cocktails very well and swizzle them better (our cocktails, in the West Indies, are drunk frothing, and the instrument with which one froths them is called a swizzle-stick) than anyone else in the house.

I measure out angostura and gin, feeling important and happy, with an uncanny intuition as to how strong I must make each separate drink.

Here then is something I can do . . . Action, they say, is more worthy than dreaming . . .

a little history

Penguin Modern Classics were launched in 1961, and have been shaping the reading habits of generations ever since.

The list began with distinctive grey spines and evocative pictorial covers – a look that, after various incarnations, continues to influence their current design – and with books that are still considered landmark classics today.

Penguin Modern Classics have caused scandal and political change, inspired great films and broken down barriers, whether social, sexual or the boundaries of language itself. They remain the most provocative, groundbreaking, exciting and revolutionary works of the last 100 years (or so).

In 2011, on the fiftieth anniversary of the Modern Classics, we're publishing fifty Mini Modern Classics: the very best short fiction by writers ranging from Beckett to Conrad, Nabokov to Saki, Updike to Wodehouse. Though they don't take long to read, they'll stay with you long after you turn the final page.

MODERN CLASSICS
www.penguinclassics.com